PAPRIKA

The Little Dust Fairy

In Search of the 'why' of Everything

written and illustrated

by

Linda Adams

To order additional copies of this book, contact:
Xlibris
844-714-8691
www.Xlibris.com
Orders@Xlibris.com

ISBN: Softcover   978-1-4363-6560-4
             EBook   978-1-4771-7781-5

Print information available on the last page

Rev. date: 08/01/2024

Dust Fairies are born in dusty corners
of people's houses.

They are very small and very happy
and seldom go on adventures.

Except for one very curious
Dust Fairy, that is.
This is her story.

Paprika's story, I mean,
because that's her name.

This is the story of Paprika
the little Dust Fairy.

In Search of the 'why' of Everything

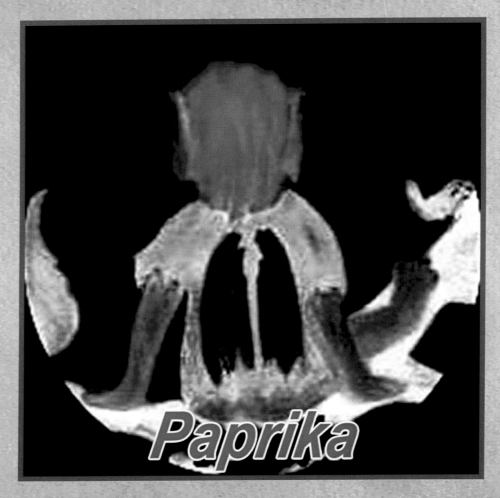

Only known photograph of Paprika
taken shortly after her birth

This is the only known photograph of Paprika taken shortly after her birth.

Unfortunately it's in black and white and not color because it was taken with a really old camera someone found in a ditch.

Some people say that if you look real close you can see that there are small pieces of dust still clinging to her hair. Other people say they can't see a thing.

I'm only telling you what I've heard. I'm just saying that there's a whole lot more I've heard about this little Dust Fairy and it's all very, very, interesting.

Yawn, stretch,
wonder, wonder, wonder
"What is this piece of stuff
that I'm under?"

"It tickles my nose
It sticks between my toes
Is it dust? Is it dust?
Is it dust?
I wonder"

"Who am I? What am I?
Why am I here?
I wonder if others like me are near.

Where is the reason?
Where is the rhyme?
What will I find out?
Will I have time?

Questions and questions
and questions and more
That's what my mind thinks
reasons are for . . ."

"Reasons are for
finding out
Questions are for
'what about?'
I'll leave right now.
I'll pack my things
Oh my, oh my,
how this dust clings."

A needle for a paddle,
a leaf for a boat
Who would ever think
a fairy could float

On and on and who did she meet . . . ?

A kind old dragon with huge big feet

A tired Paprika climbed up a stem
and fell fast asleep as the dragon
named Clem . . .

breathed his warm breath
and sweet thoughts into her ear

But then morning came
and who did she hear?

A loud old rooster
SHOUTING IN HER EAR

Shouting and saying,
"WHAT HAVE WE HERE?

LOOKS JUST LIKE A DUST FAIRY
THAT MUCH IS CLEAR."

"SEND HER TO WISE OWL
HE'LL SET HER STRAIGHT."

But then when she got there
she just had to wait . . .

"Wise owl, wise owl
I have a list
Please answer my questions
This is my wish"

"Who?" said the owl
"It's me, can't you see?"
"I have a headache and I'm tired",
said he

"Noad has the answers.
He knows it all.

He's the key master
guarding the wall."

Frevin will take you

He'll show you the way

The journey will take you

'till the end of the day

Take him some fresh fish,
and maybe a pear

There's a bucket
of green ones
right over there"

Early next morning

they woke up to see

Noad, the grand master,

holding a key.

The key in his belly
opened two drawers
and suddenly behind him
the wall had two doors . . .
which opened and opened
and now she could see

She danced and she shouted . . .

"THEY ALL LOOK LIKE ME!"

"Here is the reason
Here is the rhyme
And all that it took
was a matter of time"

Dust Fairies are born
in dusty corners of people's houses.

They are very small
and very happy
and seldom go on adventures,
but when they do
they have a really great time.

The End
. . . for now